SPACE SCOUT

SCOUTING THE UNIVERSE FOR A NEW EARTH

The Robot King
published in 2010 by
Hardie Grant Egmont
85 High Street
Prahran, Victoria 3181, Australia
www.hardiegrantegmont.com.au

PEFC

PEFC/21-31-16

*The pages of this book are printed on paper derived
from forests promoting sustainable management.*

A CiP record for this title is available from the National Library of Australia

Text copyright © 2010 H. Badger
Series, illustration and design copyright © 2010 Hardie Grant Egmont

Cover illustration by D. Mackie
Illustrated by C. Bennett
Design by S. Swingler
Typeset by Ektavo
Printed in Australia by McPherson's Printing Group

3 5 7 9 10 8 6 4

SPACE SCOUT™

THE ROBOT KING

BY **H. BADGER**

ILLUSTRATED BY **C. BENNETT**

hardie grant EGMONT

CHAPTER 1

Kip Kirby had been dreaming about this moment his whole life.

It was the last quarter of the ParticleBall Grand Final! And Kip's team, the Central City Cyborgs, had a shot at winning.

Kip played Lead Vertical Striker. It was up to him to score the winning goal. He looked up at the scoreboard.

ParticleBall was just a game to some kids. But to Kip, it was life. Well, a big part of life at least.

Kip also had a very important job as a Space Scout.

Earth was so crowded that soon it would be impossible to fit everyone in. A massive company called WorldCorp hired Space Scouts to search unknown

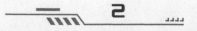

galaxies for a new home planet.

At 12, Kip was the youngest ever Space Scout. He was desperate to be the one to discover the next Earth. Every Space Scout was.

After a successful mission, Space Scouts earned one Planetary Point. For a promising discovery on a planet, two points. The Space Scout who discovered Earth 2 won a heap of amazing prizes, including the ultimate one – the Shield of Honour.

Then the points were added up and put on the Leader Board. Space Scouts always knew who was doing well and who wasn't.

'Coming your way, Kip!' yelled his

best friend Jett. Jett was the Cyborgs' 34th Assistant Vertical Striker.

Jett lobbed the ParticleBall. The metre-wide ball sailed in Kip's direction.

Kip crouched, ready to spring up and head the ball through the vertical goal. The goal was four metres off the ground!

ParticleBall was played on an indoor Field-O-Line. It looked like a round football pitch, except it was covered in fake grass as springy as a trampoline. That's how the strikers could bounce up to the goal.

The giant ParticleBall zoomed closer and closer. Eyes on the ball, Kip leapt into the air.

But at that exact moment —

Noooooooooooo!

The ParticleBall shrank to the size of a golf ball! It zinged past Kip's ear and into the foul zone.

'No-one could have got that one, Kip,' said Jett, running up behind him.

ParticleBall

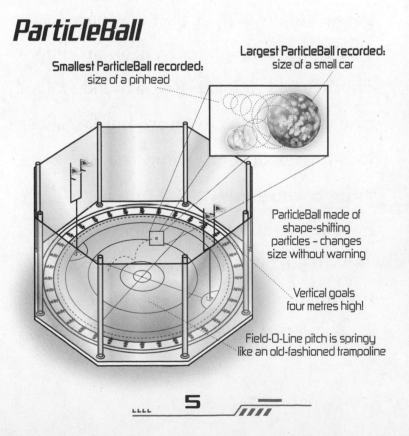

Smallest ParticleBall recorded: size of a pinhead

Largest ParticleBall recorded: size of a small car

ParticleBall made of shape-shifting particles – changes size without warning

Vertical goals four metres high!

Field-O-Line pitch is springy like an old-fashioned trampoline

'I guess,' Kip mumbled, disappointed in himself.

'You just can't tell when the ball is going to change,' Jett added, shaking his head.

ParticleBalls were made of special shape-shifting particles, so they changed size without warning. That was what made ParticleBall so difficult to play.

A whistle pierced the air.

'Team huddle!' blared the Cyborgs' RoboCoach. RoboCoach was an energetic orange robot with a built-in whistle function and wheels for feet.

Kids ran from all directions. There were two hundred players in every ParticleBall team. Wherever you went, whatever you

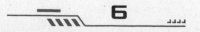

did, Earth was too crowded.

'Ten minutes left,' said RoboCoach, his glowing orange eyes fixed on Kip. 'Beating the NanoFreaks depends on our Lead Vertical Striker.'

*Ten minutes…*Kip repeated silently.

In 10 minutes, Kip was meant to be aboard his starship for a Space Scout mission! A wormhole was opening up.

Wormholes were shortcuts between galaxies. They opened and closed very quickly. Kip might miss it if he was late.

Kip's starship was called MoNa, short for Modern Navigator 4000. She had all the latest technology. But she also had the personality of a grumpy old babysitter.

Kip was her captain, but MoNa always thought she knew best.

MoNa will kill me if I'm late, Kip thought. *But if I leave now, we'll lose the Grand Final!*

Another whistle sounded. The game was back on!

I'll deal with MoNa later, Kip decided.

Jett stuck out his foot and stole the ball from a NanoFreaks player. The ball was now watermelon-sized.

'Yours!' Jett yelled, booting the ball to Kip.

Kip's eyes were welded to the ball. He raised his boot. The ball shrank to the size of a marble!

But it didn't matter. Kip's toe was under

the ball. With an almighty leap, he sprang high into the air.

Kip sailed towards the vertical goal, his eyes narrowed. He smacked the ball toward the goal.

The goalie was treading air in her anti-gravity boots, but she was too slow. The ball flew right past her, straight through the goal!

score!

Kip plummeted back down to the Field-O-Line, bouncing lightly. The crowd was going crazy!

'Affirmative! The Cyborgs have won the Grand Final!' shrieked RoboCoach.

But Kip had no time for celebrating. He

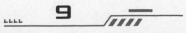

had to speed to the Intergalactic Hoverport where MoNa was docked.

She'd be seriously grumpy by now!

CHAPTER 2

Cheering Cyborgs fans flooded the Field-O-Line. But Kip headed straight for the exit. His parents pushed through the crowd towards the exit too.

Kip grabbed his SpaceCuff from his pocket, put it on his wrist and checked the time. He was supposed to be at the Hoverport *now*!

Kip used his SpaceCuff to communicate with MoNa. It had everything from a compass to a thermometer, and even a music program so Kip could remix his favourite songs.

Two minutes later, Kip met up with his parents outside the stadium.

'I packed your scouting gear,' said Kip's mum. She handed Kip his backpack.

His RocketBoard was lashed to the front. The RocketBoard was an aerodynamic skateboard made of carbon nanoparticles 600 times stronger than steel. It had mini rocket thrusters on the back.

Kip grabbed his WorldCorp spacesuit from his backpack. He pulled it on over

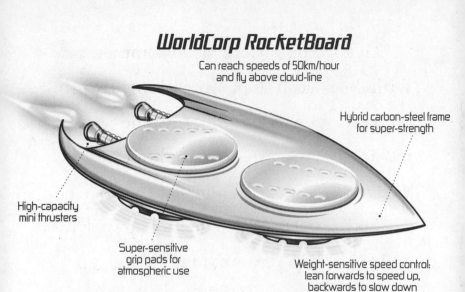

WorldCorp RocketBoard

Can reach speeds of 50km/hour
and fly above cloud-line

Hybrid carbon-steel frame
for super-strength

High-capacity
mini thrusters

Super-sensitive
grip pads for
atmospheric use

Weight-sensitive speed control:
lean forwards to speed up,
backwards to slow down

his ParticleBall uniform. Sleek and fitted, Kip's spacesuit had green boots and a helmet with sparkling red flames.

Kip clicked into the RocketBoard's grip pads. Then he flicked the RocketBoard forward. The thrusters roared.

'Remember, I don't want you hitching a ride, Kip!' called his dad. 'It's dangerous.'

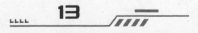

Sorry, Dad, he thought. *But how else will I make it to the Hoverport?* He was already running late.

'I'll call you!' Kip said, shooting into the air. He leant left and right to steer the RocketBoard.

Just as Kip got airborne, a wriggling WorldCorp WasteWorm flashed by. Waste-Worms were vehicles that travelled from Earth's lower atmosphere to the Hoverport and back, sucking up debris.

Kip leant forward to speed up the RocketBoard. The WasteWorm's tail was almost in reach. Kip stretched out, but the tail slipped from his fingers.

Kip sped up again and stretched until his

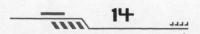

arm nearly popped off. His fingers closed around the WasteWorm's tail. He clung on tight, feet still on the RocketBoard.

Awesome, Kip thought. *A tow!*

He didn't have to hang on too long. The WasteWorm moved very fast. And the Hoverport was close by, hovering 10 kilometres above the ground.

The Hoverport looked like a giant floating carpark in the sky. Spacecraft of all kinds were docked there.

Kip saw MoNa immediately. She was black with curved thrusters and glowing lights underneath. The WasteWorm shot through the Hoverport. MoNa was almost directly above Kip.

 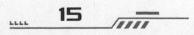

Kip flicked on his SpaceCuff. He was only four minutes late for take-off.

'Kip Kirby to MoNa 4000,' he said into it. 'Approaching now.'

'About time!' snapped MoNa. 'I'll open the landing bay.'

A hatch below MoNa's nose cone slid open. A moment later, Kip let go of the WasteWorm's tail and reached up, grabbing hold of the hatch to pull himself inside. When he was steady, he flicked the RocketBoard into his hands and stood up.

Enough death-defying stunts for today! Kip grinned, taking off his helmet.

A circular door at the end of the landing bay slid open. Kip's second-in-command

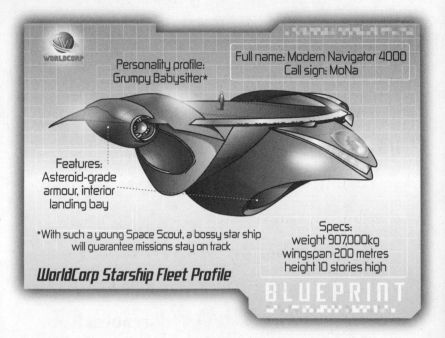

WORLDCORP

Personality profile:
Grumpy Babysitter*

Full name: Modern Navigator 4000
Call sign: MoNa

Features:
Asteroid-grade
armour, interior
landing bay

*With such a young Space Scout, a bossy star ship
will guarantee missions stay on track

Specs:
weight 907,000kg
wingspan 200 metres
height 10 stories high

WorldCorp Starship Fleet Profile

BLUEPRINT

Finbar walked through it.

'How's it going, you big ball of fluff?'
Kip called.

Although Kip and Finbar were very
different, they got along well. Finbar was
part-arctic wolf, part-human. He was
two metres tall and covered with white

fur. It was extra thick at the moment because Finbar wasn't shedding. Finbar's animal instincts really came in handy on missions.

'No time for chit-chat,' snapped a voice overhead. 'You're late!'

It was MoNa. She heard everything Kip and Finbar said.

Kip pulled a face. 'Only by four minutes! But I'll head to the bridge and download the mission brief,' he added quickly.

'You'd better,' said MoNa. 'Or else I'll tell WorldCorp about your little RocketBoard stunt.'

Kip rolled his eyes. MoNa would be such a cool starship if she weren't so bossy!

CHAPTER 3

Kip and Finbar left the landing bay together. Walking through MoNa's glowing blue corridors, they passed the Sensory Cinema. Inside, you could not only *watch* films, but touch and taste the things in the films as well.

They soon reached the bridge, MoNa's control centre. It had sloping walls and wide windows for a windshield.

In the centre of the bridge were two padded chairs. Kip and Finbar sat down. Kip waved his hand in the air above him.

Instantly, their chairs were surrounded by a cylinder of blue light. The blue light had dials, screens and a keyboard projected onto it. It was Kip's holographic consol.

He downloaded the Mission Brief.

**SPACE SCOUT
KIP KIRBY
MISSION BRIEF**

CLASSIFIED

WorldCorp's super computers have detected a wormhole leading to a planet called Arboria.

Arboria is thought to have water and aliens that are similar to humans. The planet could be an ideal Earth 2.

Kip flipped to the writing pad projected on his consol. He scribbled a message to Finbar with his finger. That way MoNa wouldn't know what he was saying.

will you be OK in the wormhole?

Finbar nodded.

Normally, Finbar was the wise, calm one. But he hated travelling through wormholes! Kip didn't want MoNa to know in case Finbar was embarrassed about it. MoNa already thought she was better than Kip and Finbar combined.

Kip programmed the wormhole's co-ordinates into his consol. As soon as he hit the Enter button, MoNa shot out of her dock at the Hoverport.

MoNa had a useful auto-pilot function. She often flew herself, but not when travelling through wormholes.

Wormholes were unpredictable, so it was dangerous for a computer to fly through them. Kip's training, intelligence and instincts were needed.

MoNa rocketed upwards, trailing flame and smoke behind her. She quickly left Earth's atmosphere behind. Soon, they were in the inky blackness of outer space.

Up ahead, Kip spotted a swirling mass of clouds streaked with red light. The wormhole was exactly where the co-ordinates said it would be.

'Engaging mega-drive,' Kip said, his hands a blur across the holographic controls. He was about to pilot MoNa through the wormhole.

At once, MoNa jumped forward. The stars became streaks outside the window. MoNa shot into the wormhole with a sucking sound. Kip's skin prickled and his eyes throbbed. They were travelling

billions of kilometres at the speed of light! It felt like riding six giant rollercoasters all at once.

A second later, MoNa popped out the other end of the wormhole.

'Are we there yet?' Finbar whimpered.

Before Kip could reply, a voice echoed through the starship. 'Welcome to Arboria's airspace, MoNa 4000,' it said warmly.

'Er, thanks,' said Kip, tapping the Communicate button on the consol.

'Please land your ship on our planet,' the male voice continued. 'We love visitors.'

He must be the galaxy's friendliest air-traffic controller, Kip thought. *He even speaks our language!*

MoNa usually didn't land on foreign planets. Instead, Kip and Finbar were teleported down by Scrambler Beams. These scrambled every particle in the body and beamed them through space. Then the particles were rearranged back into normal form on the surface of the new planet.

Kip was torn. Most planets would never invite a strange starship to land. Kip was unsure what might be waiting for him on Arboria. But the voice sounded so friendly, and it *was* his mission to explore Arboria. Plus, travelling by Scrambler was pretty uncomfortable.

'Commence landing,' Kip said finally.

'Relax! I'll guide you in with our Leech

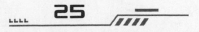

DOROTHY LYNAS

Beam,' the voice said easily.

A Leech Beam? Kip thought. *As in, the creature that sucks your blood and won't let go?*

Suddenly, a powerful force yanked MoNa downwards. She dropped closer and closer to Arboria.

Kip could see concrete buildings blanketed in an eerie haze. Everything was connected by walkways through the air. There were trees, but they had no leaves, and it looked like there was no grass anywhere.

Kip commanded MoNa to engage her landing gear. Her wheels touched down and she taxied to a stop at Arboria's Terrestrial Docking Station.

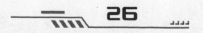

'You'll love it here,' came the air-traffic controller's voice. 'I promise, you'll never leave.'

Finbar pulled supplies from a cupboard in the bridge. 'Did you see the pollution when we landed?' he said in a low voice. 'I wonder how it got so bad.'

He grabbed extra OxyGlobes, the compact air supply Kip and Finbar used in case a planet's air wasn't safe to breathe.

With their spacesuits, helmets and OxyGlobes fitted, Kip and Finbar strode to the landing bay. Finbar hit the Exit button and MoNa's hatch slid open. Then he and Kip stepped down a folding staircase onto the planet of Arboria.

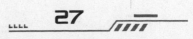

CHAPTER 4

The first thing Kip saw was a glowing, silver robot. Twice as tall as Kip, the robot had a plasma screen for a head. The screen showed a picture of a smiling man.

Looks like my grandpa trapped in a robot's body, Kip thought.

'I'm Pappy,' the robot grinned, stepping forward on its two long legs. Kip recognised

his voice. The air-traffic controller!

'Kip Kirby from planet Earth.' He shook Pappy's plastic hand.

Earth's robots were small and energetic, like RoboCoach. Their job was to make life easier for Earth's people. But this robot didn't seem like a helper model — he was more like a person than a machine.

'Finbar and I are scouting the galaxy for a new planet for our people,' said Kip.

'You must be fit and healthy for that job,' said Pappy, looking Kip up and down. 'That's great news.'

Kip shot Finbar a puzzled look.

'Can we explore your planet?' asked Finbar.

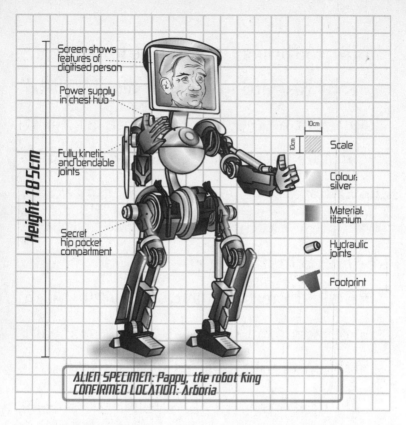

Screen shows features of digitised person

Power supply in chest hub

Fully kinetic and bendable joints

Secret hip pocket compartment

Height 185cm

10cm

10cm

Scale

Colour: silver

Material: titanium

Hydraulic joints

Footprint

ALIEN SPECIMEN: Pappy, the robot king
CONFIRMED LOCATION: Arboria

'Please do! And stay as long as you like!' Pappy said.

'How would your people feel about humans moving in with you?' Kip asked.

'That would be wonderful!' said Pappy,

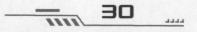

almost too brightly. 'We'd love to have you.'

Kip was getting a weird vibe from the robot, but he tried to keep on track. 'Is it true there's water here?' he asked.

'We can talk about boring stuff later,' said Pappy, waving his hand. 'Come and see my house first.'

Behind Pappy, Kip noticed the floors in the docking station were spotlessly clean. The chairs looked brand new.

Normally, docking stations were really busy with intergalactic traffic. But this one seemed deserted.

Why doesn't anyone visit Arboria? Kip wondered. *It seems OK so far.*

'This way!' said Pappy firmly, putting

one plastic arm around Kip's shoulders.

Outside the docking station, the heat hit Kip like a slap. Two hot, red suns were huge in the hazy sky.

Kip flicked his SpaceCuff to Air-Analyser mode to check the pollution.

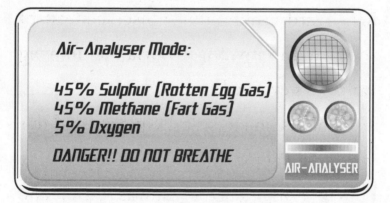

Air-Analyser Mode:

45% Sulphur (Rotten Egg Gas)
45% Methane (Fart Gas)
5% Oxygen

DANGER!! DO NOT BREATHE

AIR-ANALYSER

No wonder Kip couldn't see or hear birds tweeting. In fact, he couldn't see any animals at all. The entire population seemed to be robots.

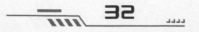

'Maybe Arboria is so polluted that only machines can live here,' whispered Finbar as they followed Pappy into the street.

Kip couldn't say just yet. But he knew it was his mission to find out.

As well as the clanking of robots' feet, Kip heard a humming noise. Instead of roads and footpaths, Arboria had moving walkways everywhere.

'Robots find it easier to get around this way,' said Pappy.

Kip noticed Arboria was dusty and completely flat, almost as if any hills had been bulldozed flat. He guessed that bumps would only trip up the robots.

Kip and Finbar stepped onto the moving

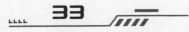

walkway outside the docking station.

The walkway sped through the streets of Arboria. Everywhere, Kip saw robots whizzing past on moving walkways. None of the robots had spotted Kip and Finbar yet. Their heads hung low, as though they were all in bad moods.

Box-shaped concrete houses lined the moving walkways. Out the front, each robot house had a pole with a purple bolt of electricity shooting out of it.

'That's where the robots recharge,' said Pappy proudly.

Kip also noticed moving 3D posters that advertised the same films and TV shows over and over.

Don't miss this!
GAME SHOWS
REPEATED ALL DAY EVERY DAY
CHANNEL 1087

See **POLICE SQUAD**
Tonight! SCREENING FOR
THE 501,347th TIME!

Boring! Kip thought. *Why aren't there any NEW movies or shows?*

A robot on a moving walkway lifted its head to look at a nearby poster. The face on its screen looked about Kip's age. It had a sad, bored look on its face.

But then the robot kid saw Finbar and

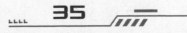

Kip. It swivelled its head in amazement.

'Know any new jokes?' yelled the kid robot.

Kip was surprised. *It seems like no-one ever visits this place,* he thought. *And the first thing this kid robot wants to know is a joke?*

The only joke Kip could think of was a lame one his dad told him. 'What's brown and sticky?' he asked.

The kid robot said nothing, but he looked excited.

'A stick,' said Kip.

'Haven't heard that one!' said the robot. It made a grinding sound, like gears in reverse. It was cracking up laughing!

'Lucky robots can't wet themselves,'

whispered Kip to Finbar. 'That guy would short-circuit.'

But Finbar didn't answer. His ears were pricking up. 'My wolf senses tell me it's about to rain,' he said slowly.

'If it rains here, there's definitely water!' Kip replied, excited. So far, Arboria didn't look like a great place for humans to live. But if there was water, there might still be hope.

I might have discovered Earth 2! he thought. *I could win the Shield of Honour.*

Then everyone would know that the youngest Space Scout was also the best.

CHAPTER 5

Kip was glad it was about to rain. But he didn't want to get soaking wet.

When he saw a fat raindrop heading right for him, he ducked out of the way.

The raindrop fell onto the moving walkway. But instead of making a splash, the raindrop sizzled when it fell.

'Does it rain boiling water here?' Kip asked Pappy.

'Why do you say that?' said Pappy, robotic eyes darting.

He's hiding something, Kip thought.

Kip glanced back at the spot where the raindrop fell. There was smoke rising from it.

'That was no ordinary raindrop,' Kip whispered to Finbar.

'Enough talking about rain,' Pappy interrupted, hurrying along the moving walkway. 'We've arrived at my house.' Pappy sounded very relieved.

Kip, Finbar and Pappy stepped off the walkway outside a pair of fancy gates.

 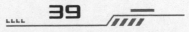

Pappy's house was a gigantic mansion. Unlike the other houses, there was a lawn with leafy trees out the front.

When Kip got close, though, he saw they were all fake. Kip was pretty sure the word 'Arboria' had something to do with trees, but there weren't *any* on this planet.

Weird, he thought.

Pappy's front door swung open. Standing in the doorway was a robot with a distinguished old man's face on its screen. The robot had a tray balanced on its hand like a butler.

'Drink, your majesty?' said the robot, bowing.

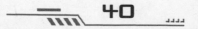

Pappy must be the king of this place! Kip thought. *Odd that he's also an air-traffic controller, then.*

Pappy took a glass filled with thick black liquid. He pressed a button on his chest and a hatch slid open. 'Nothing like a cup of oil to soothe the hinges, eh James?' said Pappy to his butler.

The robot butler offered the tray to Kip and Finbar.

I'd rather drink a brussel sprout smoothie! Kip thought.

'No, thanks,' he said out loud. 'I'd love a glass of water, though,' he added.

This'll be a quick way of finding out what the water on Arboria is like, he thought.

'Water?' James said. 'I wouldn't really recommend —'

Pappy cut in. 'There's none cold at the moment. Sorry.'

Pappy showed Kip and Finbar around his enormous house. Pappy explained that the house was a thank-you gift from the people of Arboria.

'I'm the king because I invented Digitisation,' Pappy said. 'It's a way to download a living creature's mind and install it into a robot body. So life never has to change!'

Why would you want to do that? Kip wondered. He remembered the game show repeats. The way the kid robot laughed at

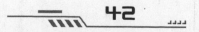

his lame joke. Life as a robot in Arboria seemed pretty dull to Kip.

'Arborians once looked like you, Kip,' Pappy added. 'But now that we're robots, we'll stay the age we were the day we got Digitised. We never have to get older!'

So that robot I met will stay a kid forever, Kip realised. *If that were me, I'd always be the youngest Space Scout. And I'd never finish school.*

'Hope you like things the way they are then,' Finbar said.

'Luckily, things on Arboria are fantastic,' Pappy agreed. Then he added, 'Would *you* like to try eternal youth, Kip?'

As if I'd ever in a million years want that! 'I've got to stay human,' Kip said quickly.

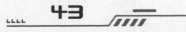

'Kip's got his job as Space Scout to think about,' Finbar explained.

'I'm asking you nicely,' Pappy smiled. For the first time, Kip noticed a cold, hard edge to his voice.

'I really need to get on with my mission,' Kip said, shaking his head. 'You said we could explore Arboria.'

'You can't leave yet,' Pappy said sweetly. 'I need a favour.' He turned to Finbar. 'I'm building a museum of curious artifacts. I'd love a lock of your fur for my collection.'

Pappy sat Finbar down. He called James and they spent ages disinfecting a pair of robotic scissors.

Why is this taking so long? Kip wondered.

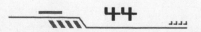

44

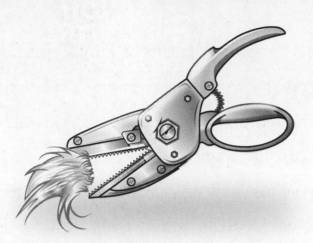

He noticed Pappy and James whispering to each other. Kip wanted to tell them to hurry up.

But then he remembered his WorldCorp Manual of Space Scouting.

SPACE SCOUT RULE 7.01
Unless in danger, a Space Scout must NEVER offend aliens.

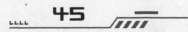

So Kip waited politely. Pappy carefully tugged a lock of fur from Finbar's tail. When he finally snipped it off, James disappeared with the fur at once. Then Pappy spent ages putting Finbar's helmet back into place.

'Thank you so much,' Pappy said finally, smiling gratefully at them.

All that over a meaningless bit of tail fluff, Kip thought.

CHAPTER 6

'I'll show you out,' said Pappy. He took Kip and Finbar to the walkway outside his house.

But the walkway was moving at triple the speed it did before.

'It's in Emergency Mode,' said Pappy, sounding surprised.

Kip saw green-and-white checked

police robots with flashing lights on top of their plasma-screen heads. They raced past, heading towards the Docking Station.

'What a fuss,' said Pappy casually as he waved goodbye. 'I hope this doesn't interfere with your mission.'

Kip and Finbar stepped onto the walkway, waving goodbye to Pappy. It whisked them away from the front gates at top speed.

'Let's find out what's going on!' Kip yelled to Finbar over the roar of sirens and clanking robot feet.

They followed the crowd to the Docking Station. A crowd of armoured robots blocked the entrance. They were made of

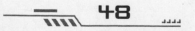

thick black plastic. Their screen heads were protected with metal cages.

'Look at MoNa,' Kip said in a low voice. She was still where Kip and Finbar had left her. But her Scrambler Beam Generator was plastered with bright orange police tape. Kip tried to push past the armoured robots.

'No-one goes in or out,' grunted the tallest armoured robot. 'There's just been a death at the Docking Station!'

'A death?' said Kip. 'Can you kill a machine?'

'It's very hard to destroy a robot,' said the armoured robot.

'But it is possible?' said Kip.

The robot nodded grimly. 'The death of the maintenance robot is shocking. It was just minding its own business, cleaning near the foreign starship.'

The foreign starship? Uh-oh, thought Kip. *What if they think MoNa's got something to do with it?*

He decided that now was a good time to act confidently. 'I'm the captain of the foreign starship,' said Kip boldly.

'I'm his second-in-command,' said Finbar.

'We need to see whoever's in charge of the investigation,' Kip said.

A plastic hand clamped down on Kip's shoulder. Another clamped on Finbar's.

Kip turned around and saw a police robot standing behind them.

'I'm in charge,' said the robot. 'And I'm arresting your companion for murder.'

'Why?' said Kip, outraged.

'The maintenance robot was found with a white furball in his circuitry,' said the police robot. 'The circuitry caught fire, destroying the robot's memory.'

The police robot yanked Finbar's arm and dragged him towards the moving walkway.

'I'm innocent,' said Finbar in a dignified voice.

'Oh yeah?' said the police robot. 'Who else around here's got thick, white fur?'

Electric shackles
attached by
laser beams

He grabbed Finbar's gloved paws and cuffed them to his feet with a pair of buzzing electric shackles.

'I'm not shedding at the moment,' Finbar explained calmly. 'It *can't* be *my* fur.'

'Whatever you say,' snorted the police robot, dragging Finbar away.

'Where are you taking him?' Kip yelled, his panic rising. But the police robots didn't answer. Within seconds, they were gone.

'They'll throw him into the Acid Lake. That's what happens to murderers,' laughed the guard robot.

Acid Lake? Kip shivered. *That does not sound good.* He raced to the walkway and jumped on. His first thought was to go to

Pappy for help.

But although Pappy had seemed friendly, there was also something creepy about him.

I'll follow those police robots instead and find Finbar without Pappy's help, Kip decided. He knew it was important to follow his instincts on a mission.

But he had no idea which way the robots had gone. Moving walkways branched off in all directions, each crammed with robots.

There was only one way Kip could find out. He had to call MoNa on his SpaceCuff. She could track Finbar using her DNA Tracker. The DNA Tracker scanned the air for traces of Kip and Finbar's DNA.

Of course, Kip would have to tell MoNa

that Finbar was missing.

MoNa thought Kip was too young for the job of Space Scout. So he hated admitting to MoNa that the mission was going badly. But he hated the idea of losing Finbar even more.

'Come in, MoNa,' said Kip into his SpaceCuff.

'What now?' said MoNa wearily. 'This mission has been horrible. First a robot sneaked into my landing bay. Then there was all that orange tape gumming up my Scrambler Beam. It'll take ages to clean it.'

'Listen, MoNa,' Kip interrupted. He didn't have time for her complaints. 'Finbar is missing. I need to you to find him.'

'What?' MoNa screeched. 'I'll track him immediately. There's no way I'm staying here longer than I have to. You're lucky I haven't left already.'

A moment later, MoNa came through. 'I've got a trace of fur heading south-west.'

Using his SpaceCuff's compass feature, Kip checked which way south-west was. Then he jumped onto the walkway heading in that direction.

'Make sure you find him, Kip,' said MoNa through the SpaceCuff. 'I don't trust these robots.'

CHAPTER 7

The moving walkway sped away from the docking station. Kip found himself leaving the concrete buildings of Arboria behind. There were no other robots on the walkways. Wherever Kip was heading, it seemed to be deserted.

Flat, grey ground stretched out in every direction. There were twisted grey trees

without leaves. Black rain clouds hung low in the sky. *I hope those clouds aren't full of burning rain*, Kip thought. Then suddenly, his brain made a connection.

The robot guard said that Finbar would be thrown in the Acid Lake! And the rain Kip had seen was burning hot.

It's acid rain! Kip thought. *And that fills the Acid Lake!* He checked his SpaceCuff for information on acid rain.

SPACE DICTIONARY

Acid Rain: Poisonous rain caused by pollution. Acid rain is burning hot, kills leaves and plants and can damage buildings.
WARNING: Can be fatal to humans and animals.

DICTIONARY

It all fits! Kip thought. Arboria may have once been covered in leafy trees. But now the leaves were all dead because of the acid rain.

Arboria's terrible pollution must have caused the acid rain, figured Kip.

But right then, pollution wasn't Kip's main worry. Finding Finbar was. Kip couldn't imagine a Space Scout mission without Finbar. But more importantly than that, they were friends.

Kip soon spotted the Acid Lake. It was huge with fluorescent waves lapping a dusty shore. Beside it, Kip saw a ramshackle old hut.

Kip jumped off the walkway. In the dust

among some robot footprints, Kip spotted a trail of pawprints!

They've got to be Finbar's, Kip thought.

A chill crept over Kip. The pawprints led straight towards the Acid Lake.

Heart pumping, Kip followed the pawprints. Soon, he was standing right on the edge of the toxic lake. The pawprints stopped.

Kip tried to yell Finbar's name, but no words came out.

His mind flooded with memories of Finbar. His wise, gentle face. How he calmed MoNa down when she got angry. The way he chased his tail to make Kip laugh.

Kip wanted to howl, but it didn't feel right. Space Scouts were meant to be grown-ups. And grown-ups didn't burst into tears whenever they felt like it.

Kip sat on the shore with his head in his hands. His eyes were close to the dusty ground.

Is that...another pawprint? Kip thought slowly. He leapt up, blinking his eyes to clear the dust away.

How could he have missed it before? A little way off, the trail of pawprints kept going. It led from the lake to the ramshackle hut.

With gritted teeth, Kip marched to the hut. He hammered on the door.

'Finbar?' Kip yelled.

Slowly, the door of the hut creaked open. Inside, it was totally dark.

'I knew you'd come,' said a familiar voice. Then a glowing white shape loomed out of the darkness. It was Pappy!

Kip gasped. What was Pappy doing way out here?

Pappy's strong robotic arms gripped Kip's wrists. He dragged Kip inside the hut and slammed the door.

'Where's Finbar?' Kip demanded.

'I'll show you,' Pappy said, crouching down. He pulled open a trapdoor in the floor. Through the trapdoor, Kip could see a staircase leading to a dark basement.

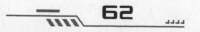

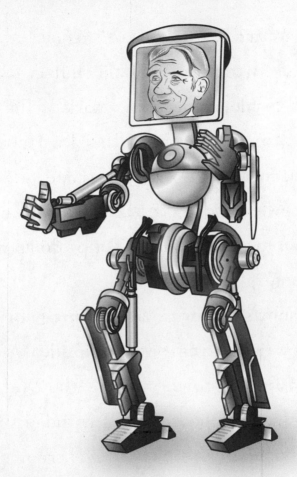

Pappy flicked a switch and white light flooded the basement. Then he pushed Kip down the stairs.

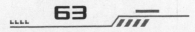

It was a lab, full of high-tech machinery! No-one would ever guess such a place could be hidden inside a wonky old hut.

The biggest machine had two chairs joined by a thick silver cable. Above each chair was a metal cap about the size of a human head. Sticking out of each cap was a strange globe-shaped object.

'Where's Finbar?' asked Kip again.

'This is where I invented Digitisation,' said Pappy, ignoring him. 'I thought I'd solved my people's problems. I had such high hopes.'

Kip glanced around. The lab was creepy, and Pappy wasn't making sense. Worst of all, there was no sign of Finbar.

BANG!

Pappy slammed the trapdoor shut and turned to Kip with a threatening smile on his face.

'No-one leaves Arboria,' Pappy said coldly.

CHAPTER 8

'*What?*' Kip exclaimed. 'Is this to do with that robot dying?'

'I *know* you had nothing to do with that,' said Pappy softly.

For a moment, Kip stared at Pappy. Then a terrible thought occurred to him.

'Finbar's fur!' Kip yelled. 'It wasn't a museum piece. You planted it on that

maintenance robot so everyone would think the death was Finbar's fault.'

Pappy pulled Kip over to one of the chairs with the metal cap and thick silver cables.

'But *why?*' said Kip.

Pappy pressed Kip's shoulders so he sat down in the chair. Buzzing shackles closed over Kip's wrists, trapping him.

'I had to find a way to make you stay,' said Pappy. 'I could see you hated Arboria as much as I do. You wanted to get away.' Pappy sat down in the chair next to Kip.

'You hate Arboria?' said Kip. 'But you're the king. You *made* Arboria this way.'

For a moment, Pappy looked sad. 'Our planet was once covered in green leafy trees, but the pollution got so bad that everything died.'

Pappy pulled down the metal cap above his chair. He fitted the cap onto his own head. 'I thought turning everyone into

robots would save us from dying off too,' he continued. 'I didn't realise how horrible it would be to never change or grow old.'

Kip remembered the kid robot's desperation for new jokes. The repeated game shows. The sad robots he saw on the moving walkways.

'I've waited so long for someone like you,' said Pappy. 'No-one has visited in such a long time. Everyone in our galaxy knows Arboria is too toxic.'

There was a whirring sound. The metal cap above Kip was being lowered automatically. It dropped onto Kip's head with a clang.

'Ow,' Kip said crossly.

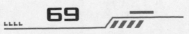

'I'm going to download myself into your body,' said Pappy. 'And when my butler James finishes locking up my house, he will take over Finbar's body. Then we're taking your starship and leaving Arboria forever.'

'You can't!' said Kip, horrified.

'I can,' said Pappy. 'It's a reversal of the Digitisation process. I simply press the Download button.'

For the first time, Kip noticed a silver remote control in Pappy's pincer. The control had a big red button on it.

Desperately, Kip tried to rip his hands out of the shackles. But it was no use. He couldn't move.

With a soft click, Pappy pressed the red button. There was a hum from Pappy's chair.

Pappy wriggled in his chair with excitement.

'A real body again,' he babbled. 'Pity it is a child's, but I'll get used to tha—'

Suddenly, Pappy fell silent.

The globe on top of Pappy's metal cap was flashing on and off. The way it flashed reminded Kip of something being saved onto a memory stick.

The machine's sucking Pappy's mind out of his head and storing it in the globe, Kip thought.

Strangely, Kip's own mind felt totally

normal. *The machine must download Pappy's mind before it uploads on mine!*

If Kip was right, it meant Pappy would be just a body without a mind for a least a few seconds. Pappy must have been too excited to think things through properly.

If I can get out of these shackles, I've got a chance to save myself and Finbar, Kip told himself.

He looked again at the shackles. They were bright pink, buzzing bands of electricity across his wrist.

These are electric, thought Kip. *Maybe I can short-circuit them!*

A plan popped into his head. He'd recently installed a Handshake Buzzer

program on his SpaceCuff. When it was switched on, the buzzer gave a mild electric shock to anyone he shook hands with.

Space Scouts were forbidden to have prank software. *But sometimes it pays to bend the rules*, Kip laughed to himself.

With an awkward twist of his wrist, he switched on his SpaceCuff and engaged Handshake Buzzer mode.

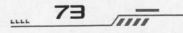

The electric current was mild, but it was enough to cause a power surge in the shackles.

With a shower of sparks, the shackles switched off. Kip was free! Leaping up from the chair, he ripped off his metal cap.

Pappy didn't move. He couldn't. His mind was stored in the globe!

Kip raced for the stairs. He was about to escape when he remembered something Pappy said.

James will take over Finbar's body...

Pappy was planning to download James's mind into Finbar! And that meant Finbar had to be nearby.

CHAPTER 9

Got to search the lab, Kip said to himself.

But something worried him. James could be on his way here to take Finbar's body. It would be dangerous to leave Pappy's mind stored in the metal cap.

Safer to download Pappy into something I can then hide, Kip decided.

Kip scanned Pappy's lab for ideas.

Behind Pappy's chair was a desk with a model robot on it. It looked like Pappy and the other robots on Arboria, except mini. Its screen displayed an emoticon instead of a proper face.

A prototype from when Pappy invented Digitisation? Perfect!

Kip grabbed the small, flimsy robot. He put it on his chair. Then he balanced the metal cap on the robot's head. It was much too big. Kip crossed his fingers that the technology would work anyway.

He raced over to Pappy. His screen head was blank, like a sleeping computer. Kip prised the remote control out of Pappy's hand. Kip knew Pappy couldn't suddenly

come to life. All the same, he held his breath.

If I press the button again, Pappy's mind should end up in the toy robot, Kip figured.

He screwed his eyes shut and pressed the button. He heard the same low hum as before. He opened his eyes.

The mini-robot was waving its tiny hands in the air. The emoticon on its screen was *not* a smiley face.

'I will not stand for this!' the little robot chirped.

Grinning, Kip scooped the

mini-robot up. The robot kicked its legs and waved its arms even more.

'You're strong for something so small,' Kip said. 'I better put you away before you hurt someone.'

Pappy squeaked. He sounded like a furious rubber duck!

There was a door at one end of the lab. Kip flung it open, thinking it was a storage cupboard.

But instead, the door led to a small room full of cages. And in the nearest one, Kip spotted Finbar.

'I thought you were dead!' Kip said, relief flooding through him.

'You'll *both* be dead if I've got anything

to do with it!' squealed Pappy.

'What did you do to him?' said Finbar, stifling a wolfish chuckle.

'I'll explain later,' said Kip, unlatching Finbar's cage.

In a second, Finbar was free. His tail wagged back and forth like crazy.

Kip shoved Pappy into the cage and slammed the door shut.

'Don't you dare leave me here!' came Pappy's shrill voice.

Kip and Finbar sped up the stairs and out of the basement.

'Gotta run!' Kip yelled over his shoulder. Speeding outside, he flicked on his SpaceCuff and called MoNa. Would the robot guards let MoNa leave the docking station? And what if MoNa hadn't cleared the tape from her Scrambler Beam Generator?

'Can you get airborne, MoNa? We need two Scrambler Beams…urgently!'

When MoNa responded, she sounded seriously annoyed. 'I've only been ready for *hours,*' she said.

Twenty seconds later, two beams of hot white light shot down from the sky. Kip and Finbar each stepped into a Scrambler.

No robot guard would dare mess with MoNa when she's angry, Kip grinned, stepping into the beam.

Finbar whimpered softly. He hated the

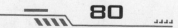

Scrambler Beam. Kip didn't like it much either – it always felt like his heart, lungs and stomach were being shuffled around like a pack of cards.

Still, I'd do anything to get out of this place, Kip thought, closing his eyes.

When he opened them again, Kip found himself sprawled on the floor of MoNa's landing bay. Finbar lay quivering beside him. Kip stood up, ripped off his helmet and brushed down his spacesuit.

'So, the evil robots didn't get you after all?' said MoNa gruffly.

Kip laughed. He was back safe with his mind still inside his body. Nothing MoNa said could upset him.

'Don't forget you've got a report to file,' added MoNa.

Almost nothing, Kip groaned silently.

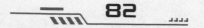

CHAPTER 10

From the landing bay, it was a quick walk back to the bridge where Kip would file his report. On the way there, Kip and Finbar passed the Sensory Cinema again.

Outside the Sensory Cinema was a poster made of a paper-thin plasma screen. Every day, it advertised a different, brand-new movie. Today's was called *Volcano Quest*.

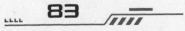

Kip nodded his head at the poster. He wanted to watch it, but he didn't want MoNa to know.

'What about your report?' Finbar mouthed.

Kip shrugged. MoNa could find them if she really wanted to.

Kip and Finbar slipped silently into the Sensory Cinema. They felt their way through the darkness until they each found a Sensomatic Seat.

The cinema sensed Kip and Finbar were sitting down. The movie started playing automatically.

Volcano Quest starred a guy called Bear Robinson, Kip's favourite adventure hero.

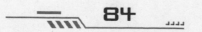

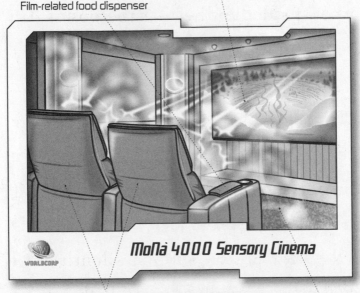

Film-related food dispenser

Films smells projected into air

MoNa 4000 Sensory Cinema

WORLDCORP

Arcmchairs made from high-quality Martian leather

Sensor pads
re-create environment

When the movie began, Bear was rafting
down molten lava.

The further Bear got into the volcano,
the more Kip and Finbar's seats smoked.
The smell of lava and smoke wafted from
the screen. Special sensor pads under the

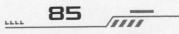

carpet made the floor of the cinema feel like it was liquid.

'Exactly like being there,' Kip whispered to Finbar.

'I'm glad we're not, after what we've been through,' said Finbar.

Bear Robinson made it to the middle of the volcano. He grabbed a packet of marshmallows and toasted them over the molten lava.

At that exact moment, Kip and Finbar's arm rests popped open. Inside, were hot toasted marshmallows for them to eat. It was the best part of the whole movie.

When the credits started, Kip stood up. 'That was awesome,' he said to Finbar. 'And

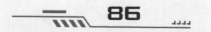

next time we go on a Space Scout mission, there'll be a totally different movie.'

'Not like Arboria,' said Finbar.

For a moment, Kip imagined what it would be like if his whole world stayed exactly as it was right at that second.

He'd never turn 13. He'd be in the ParticleBall junior league forever. He'd still travel to other galaxies on Space Scout missions. But he'd never get stronger, taller, smarter or braver.

'I like my life now,' said Kip, as they left the Sensory Cinema. 'But I don't want things to be exactly the same tomorrow.'

'If you don't file your report soon, your life won't be the same tomorrow!' said

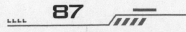

MoNa snappily. 'I'll tell WorldCorp and you'll lose your job as Space Scout.'

'Don't get your circuits in a twist, MoNa,' grinned Kip. 'I'll do it right now.'

He and Finbar hurried through MoNa's glowing blue corridors until they reached the bridge.

Kip settled into the padded captain's chair in the middle of the room. He touched the air above the chair. Instantly, the blue cylinder with his holographic consol formed around him.

He touched a button labelled Captain's Log, projected into the air.

A floating holographic keyboard appeared and Kip started typing.

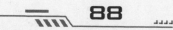

CAPTAIN'S LOG
Arboria

Climate: Polluted. Regular, burning hot acid rain showers. For complete protection, I recommend a lead umbrella.

Population: Human-like beings transformed into robots through Digitisation. Robots can't grow up, change or have new ideas. They are more bored than I was when Mum took me to a space ballet concert.

National pastimes: Watching old movies and game shows, telling bad jokes.

Summary: Arboria has plenty of water, but it's toxic. Earth's people should NOT move to Arboria and Digitise. Unless they enjoy watching *The Billion Dollar Question* 51,672 times!

KIP KIRBY, SPACE SCOUT #50

Once Kip had filed his report, he clicked on the Planetary Points Leader Board. Kip didn't say anything to Finbar, but he was a bit nervous waiting for it to load.

What if one of the other Space Scouts discovered the perfect planet while I was defending myself against body-snatching robots?

The Leader Board results popped up. For Kip's mission to Arboria, he'd earned one point. In the last 24 hours, Space Scout #34 had earned two points for finding soil a bit like Earth's. But whether any food would grow in it was unknown.

It seemed no-one had found the perfect planet yet. Kip was ranked somewhere in the middle of the board.

Not bad, he thought. *But I'd prefer to be on top.*

Kip had helped the Central City Cyborgs get to the top of the ParticleBall ladder.

The Leader Board would take more time. But Kip knew he'd get there — someday soon.

THE END

HAVE YOUR OWN REAL LIFE ADVENTURE AT DREAMWORLD AND WHITEWATER WORLD!

TOWER II OF TERROR

Run riot in *Dreamworld's Nick Central* with your favourite Nick characters, take a walk on the wild side on *Tiger Island* or come face to face with Australian Wildlife. Tiny tots can ride the Big Red Car in *Wiggles World*, while big kids face their fears on the *Big 6 Thrill Rides*.

Then slide into *WhiteWaterWorld* and cool off at Nickelodeon *Pipeline Plunge*, splash about in the *Cave of Waves* and ride some of the hottest waterslides on the planet!